Y0-DLE-684

United States Regions

Appalachian
Region

Ellen K. Mitten

Rourke Educational Media
rourkeeducationalmedia.com

Scan for Related Titles
and Teacher Resources

Before & After Reading Activities

Level: **Q** Word Count: **912 Words**
100th word: *mountains* page 8

Before Reading:

Building Academic Vocabulary and Background Knowledge

Before reading a book, it is important to tap into what your child or students already know about the topic. This will help them develop their vocabulary, increase their reading comprehension, and make connections across the curriculum.

1. Look at the cover of the book. What will this book be about?
2. What do you already know about the topic?
3. Let's study the Table of Contents. What will you learn about in the book's chapters?
4. What would you like to learn about this topic? Do you think you might learn about it from this book? Why or why not?
5. Use a reading journal to write about your knowledge of this topic. Record what you already know about the topic and what you hope to learn about the topic.
6. Read the book.
7. In your reading journal, record what you learned about the topic and your response to the book.
8. After reading the book complete the activities below.

Content Area Vocabulary
Read the list. What do these words mean?

cash crops
coal
culture
dulcimer
forests
frontier
lumber
mining
pioneers
reclamation
rural
subsistence farmers
tourism

After Reading:

Comprehension and Extension Activity

After reading the book, work on the following questions with your child or students in order to check their level of reading comprehension and content mastery.

1. Why is this region mostly rural? (Asking questions)
2. Why is poverty common in this region of the United States? (Infer)
3. How did the Cherokees help the settlers who lived in this region? (Asking questions)
4. If the Cherokees and settlers lived in peace for many years, why did the U.S. government seize Cherokee land? (Infer)
5. In what ways do you think pioneers changed the Appalachian region? (Asking questions)

Extension Activity

Tourism is important for the economy in the Appalachian region. Create a poster or a 45 second commercial to attract people to visit this beautiful area of the United States. Include things to do, sights to see, and historical facts to draw people to this area.

Table of Contents

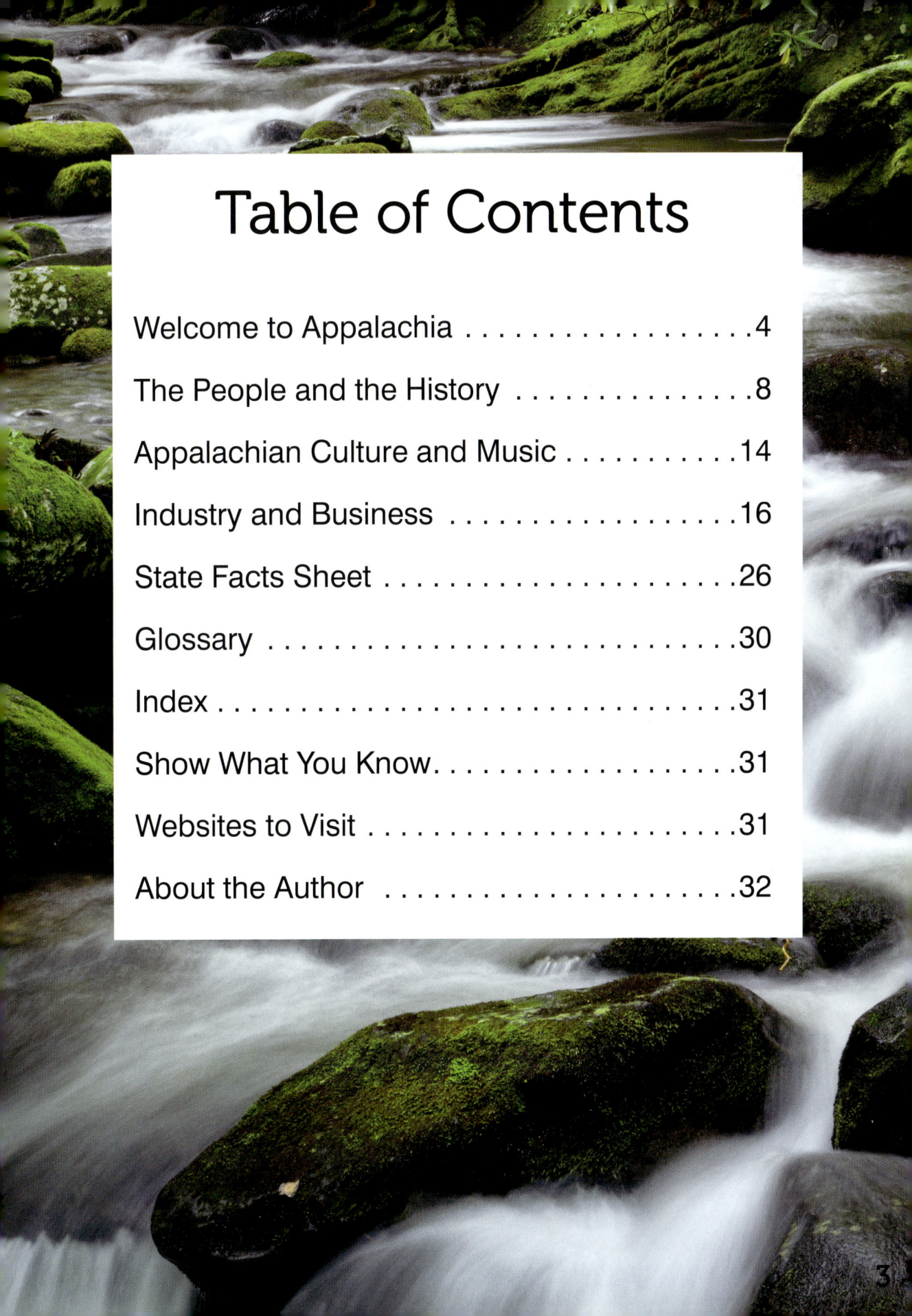

Welcome to Appalachia 4

The People and the History 8

Appalachian Culture and Music 14

Industry and Business 16

State Facts Sheet 26

Glossary 30

Index 31

Show What You Know. 31

Websites to Visit 31

About the Author 32

Welcome to Appalachia

The Appalachian region of the United States follows the peaks of the Appalachian Mountain range from Northern Alabama to Southern New York. The Appalachian region has a population of around 25 million people. Many of these people live in **rural** areas.

Rural Mountain Cabin in the Appalachian Mountains

The states that make up the Appalachian region are part of New York, Pennsylvania, West Virginia, Virginia, Kentucky, Georgia, North Carolina, Tennessee, South Carolina, Ohio, and Alabama.

Southern Appalachian Mountains

The Appalachian region is one of the most beautiful places in North America, with pleasant green valleys and tree-covered mountains. The Appalachian Mountain range includes the Allegheny Mountains, the Cumberland Mountains, the Blue Ridge Mountains, and the Great Smoky Mountains.

The entire Appalachian range contains huge **forests** made up of hardwood and conifer trees. The wet environment includes streams, waterfalls, and the thick vegetation. White clouds hug the peaks of the mountains and produce mountain mist.

Waterfall in the Blue Ridge Mountains of North Carolina

The Great Smoky Mountains were the ancestral home of the Cherokees. The Cherokee name for the mountain range was Shaconaque, which translates to place of blue smoke.

The People and the History

The first Appalachians were the Cherokee Native America tribe. The Cherokee were a self-reliant, woodland tribe who worked hard to survive in the mountains.

British, French, and Spanish settlers were some of the first people to come to the South. They started arriving in the eighteenth century. But they weren't the first to call the region home. Native peoples had lived there since prehistoric times.

Cherokee Indian

Each Cherokee household lived off the land by hunting game, farming corn, squash, and beans, and gathering plants and berries.

In the early 1700s, Scotch-Irish, German, and British descendants settled in the Appalachian region. Many of these poor immigrants came to the mountains hoping to farm their own small plots of land.

A typical log cabin was built by hand. The cabin had a central chimney and one or two rooms. Today, these log cabins symbolize the heritage and independence of the mountain people.

Tobacco was a major crop during the 1700s and often used to barter for other items.

Like the Cherokee, the European settlers established a **culture** based on living off the land. Almost all of the settlers were **subsistence farmers**, meaning that their farms provided everything that their family needed to live. The farmers planted wheat, corn, and hay. They raised chickens, sheep, hogs, and cows. They also grew tobacco and sorghum, a type of sugar plant, as **cash crops**.

For many years, the Cherokee and settlers lived in peace. The Appalachian mountain range served as a barrier between the eastern states and the west **frontier**, which limited the number of settlers in the region. However, in 1769, Daniel Boone led an expedition through the Cumberland Gap. This trail became the way for **pioneers** to reach the western frontier. As new pioneers spread west, competition for farmland grew.

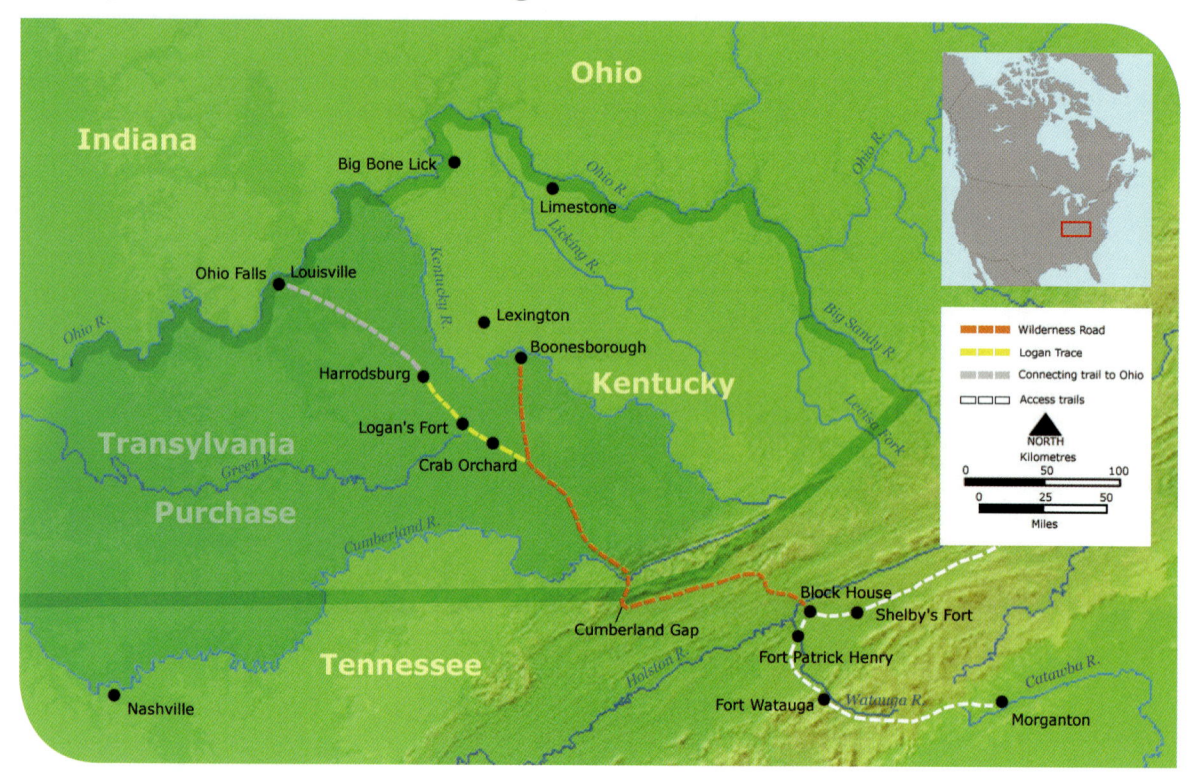

The Cumberland Gap is at the junction of Tennessee, Kentucky, and West Virginia.

The pioneer trail through the Cumberland Gap was first discovered by bison looking to eat at the mountain salt mines. The Cherokee followed the bison trail, and the frontiersmen followed the Cherokee, forging a path from east to west.

Cherokee Indians ride with wagons packed on their way to the Oklahoma reservation.

The relationship between the Cherokee and the settlers deteriorated. The U.S. government seized Cherokee land and forced the people to an Oklahoma reservation. This relocation from the mountains was known as the Trail of Tears. Some Cherokee refused to leave, forming the Eastern Band of Cherokee.

Appalachian Culture and Music

The settlers had adopted the many traditional Cherokee crafts, including basket weaving, pottery, jewelry making, sewing, corn husking, and rag doll making. The settlers also added their own art of whittling, furniture making, quilting, music, and storytelling.

Music was an important part of life for the Appalachian settlers. String instruments, such as the guitar, banjo, fiddle, and **dulcimer** were used to create soft, sweet sounds and the fast vibrant music, used for square dancing and clog dancing. Clog dancing developed from the different step dances of the English, Irish, German, and Cherokee.

Dulcimer

Storytelling was another form of entertainment born in the mountains. Today, Jonesborough, Tennessee is considered to be the storytelling capital of the world.

In the 1940s, Richard Thomas Chase, an American folklorist, wrote down as many stories as he could find from old Appalachian storytellers. He captured the spirit of the tales so future generations could hear the stories of their ancestors.

Elderberry Sauce

Ingredients:

4 cups elderberries

½ cup sugar

Directions:

Heat berries until juice runs. Add sugar and cook until liquid boils and crystals dissolve. Pour mixture into jar and let firm. Then slice and serve.

Industry and Business

The Appalachian people were mostly isolated farmers and craftspeople. But in the late 1800s, railroads opened up huge tracks of land to the industrial northeast and midwestern regions. Companies soon entered Appalachia to extract its natural resources. These industries provided jobs, but also hurt the environment.

The mountains were full of hickory, oak, locust, pine, walnut, maple, cherry, ash, birch and yellow poplar trees, making the region attractive to the lumber industry, which moved the logs by train for export.

The **lumber** industry was the first major industry in the Appalachian region. Large logging companies moved into North Carolina, Tennessee, Virginia, and West Virginia to take control of this resource. By the early 1900s, hardwood lumber was an important part of the economy.

However, the logging companies clear-cut the trees, leaving behind bare land prone to flooding. Many communities washed away. Today, some areas in Southern Appalachia still suffer from flooding due to clear-cutting.

Coal miners pose for a picture outside a mine in Pittsburgh, Pennsylvania.

The mountains in Appalachia were filled with **coal**. In the late 1800s, coal became an essential fuel for trains, factories, and homes. Soon after, major **mining** industries entered Appalachia. The mountains became one of the largest sources of coal in the world.

Mining companies hired Appalachian farmers, European immigrants, and African Americans from the deep South. Although mining was profitable for the companies, it was dangerous for the miners. Many men were injured in the mines or died from breathing in the black coal dust.

The boom in coal production continued from 1880 to 1930. But after World War II, mining became more mechanized and fewer workers were needed. Today, mines in West Virginia and Kentucky employ only a small number of people.

Since the 1970s, mining companies in Appalachia have used mountain top removal to get coal. The process makes coal mining easier, but it destroys the environment.

By the early 1960s, the demise of the coal and lumber industries left the Appalachian region in extreme poverty. President Lyndon Johnson established the Appalachian Regional Commission in 1965 to improve the economy.

The Commission's first goal was to create a 3,500 mile (5,632 kilometer) highway network to reduce isolation in Appalachia. Today, this road system connects Appalachian communities to national and international markets.

The Commission also aims to improve communication systems and promote education. The number of counties below the poverty level has reduced by more than half since the commission started.

Appalachian farmhouse in the mountains of West Virginia.

High School Completion Rates in Appalachia, 2007–2011
(County Rates)

A high school completion rate is the percentage of persons ages 25 and over with a high school diploma or more. The map uses natural breaks in the distribution to organize the data into groups of common values.

U.S. average = 85.4%
Appalachian average = 83.5%

Completion Rate
- 56.1% - 70.9%
- 71.0% - 77.7%
- 77.8% - 84.0%
- 84.1% - 92.9%

(Natural Breaks Classification)

Map Created: October 2013
Data Source: U.S. Census Bureau, American Community Survey, 2007–2011

APPALACHIAN REGIONAL COMMISSION

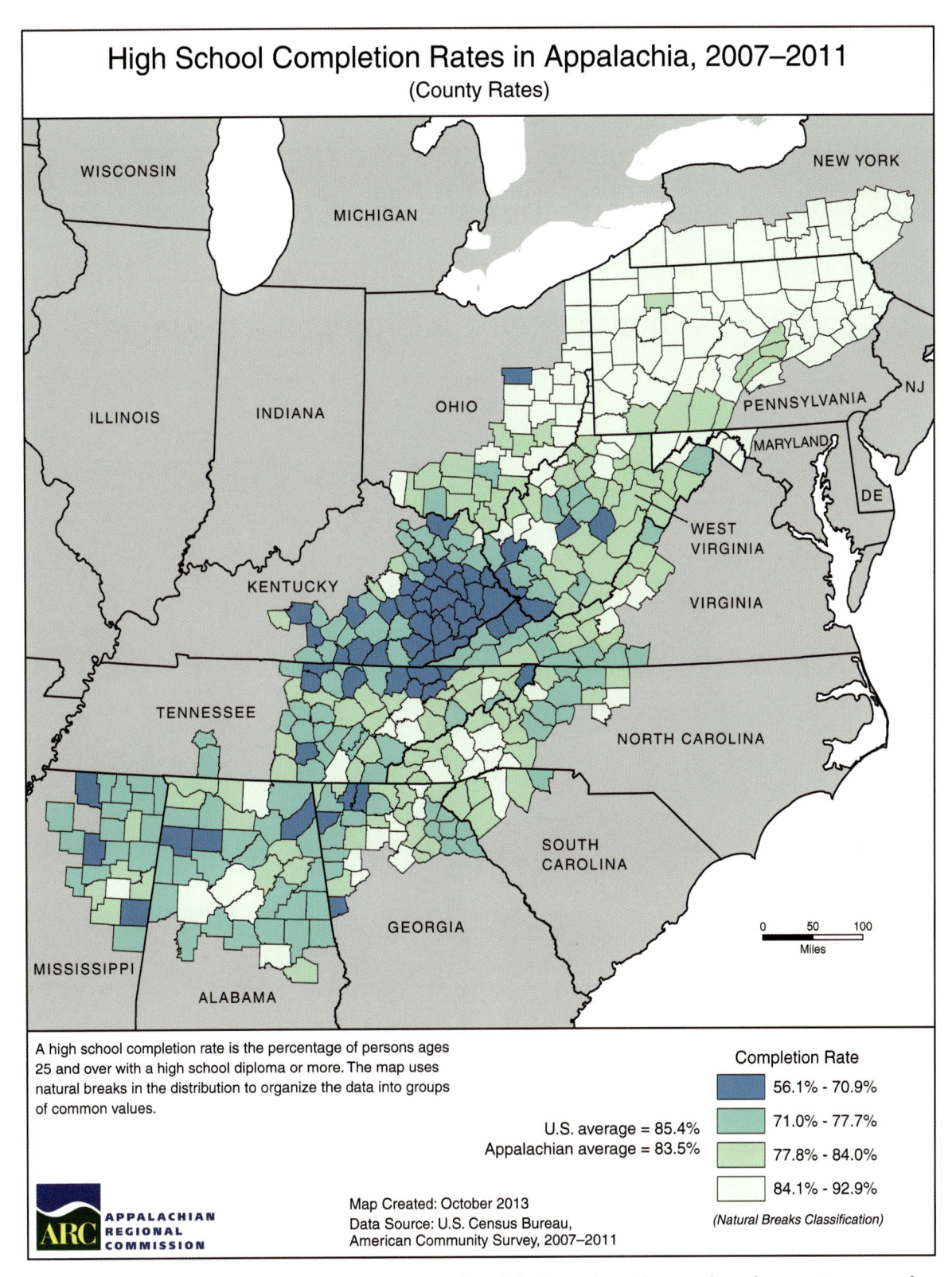

Assistance is needed to improve the high school graduation rates and increase the number of students who go to college.

In addition to economic progress, areas impacted by lumbering and mining need repair. Appalachian states are working to protect the surface and groundwater supplies and encourage **tourism**. The Commission also contributes to these **reclamation** efforts, which increase job opportunities that enhance and preserve the region.

The Appalachian National Scenic Trail, completed in 1937, is a 2,168 mile (3,489 kilometer) footpath that extends along the mountains of the Appalachian range, reaching from Maine to Georgia. Each year, 2 to 3 million people hike part of the trail.

The Shenandoah National Park encompasses part of the Blue Ridge Mountains. More than 200 bird species make their home in the park.

The spirit of the Appalachian culture as both a people and a place is still alive today. The importance of family, traditions, music, storytelling, and craftsmanship are part of mountain life. The mountains and cabins are timeless aspects of the American landscape. To protect the future of this special place, Appalachians will need to conserve the beauty of their landscape and encourage positive use of their natural resources.

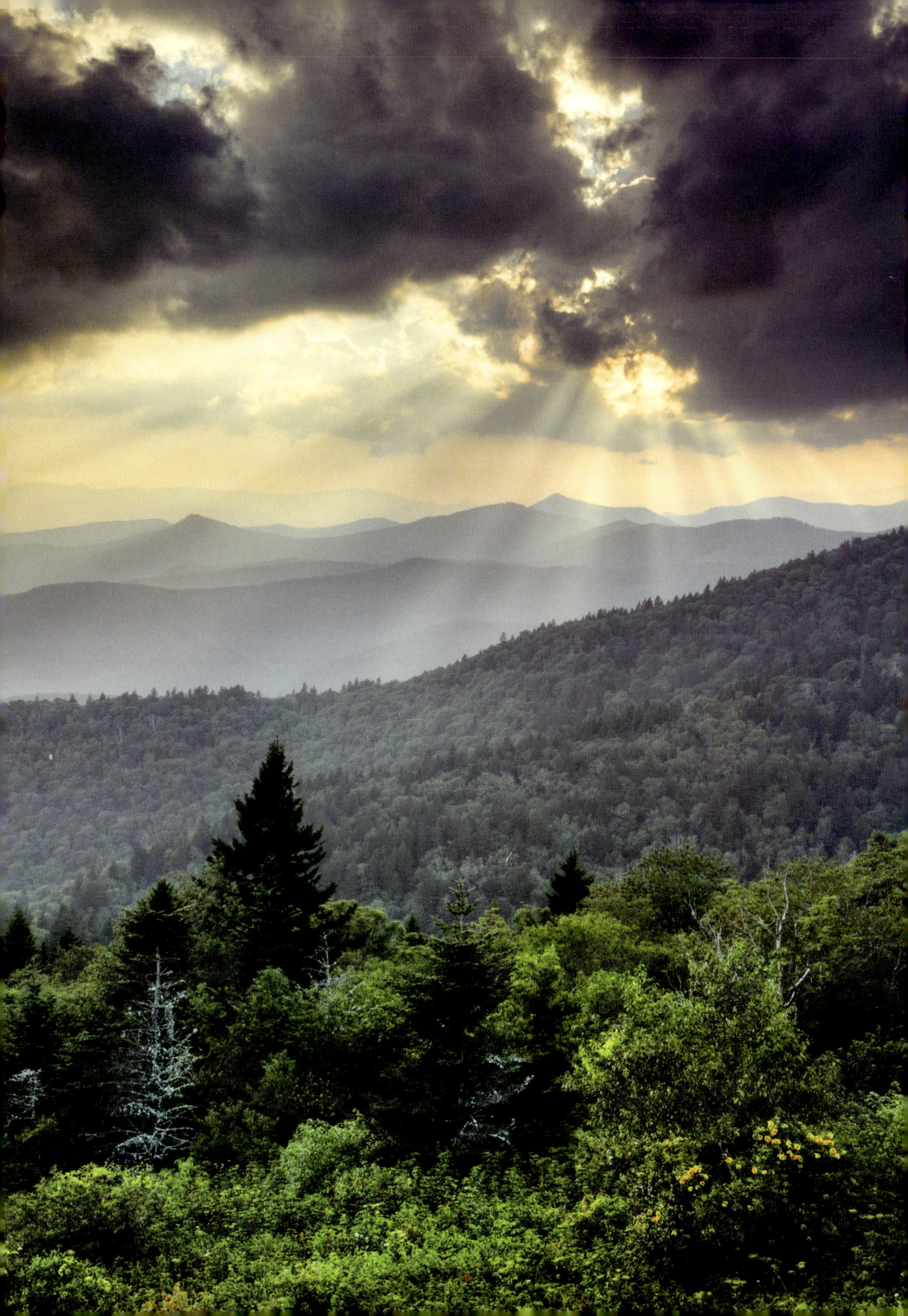

State Facts Sheet

New York

Motto: Excelsior (which means "Ever Upward.")
Nickname: Empire State
Capital: Albany
Known for: Banking, Skyscrapers, and Forests
Fun Fact: New York City was the first capital of the United States. George Washington took his oath as president there in 1789.

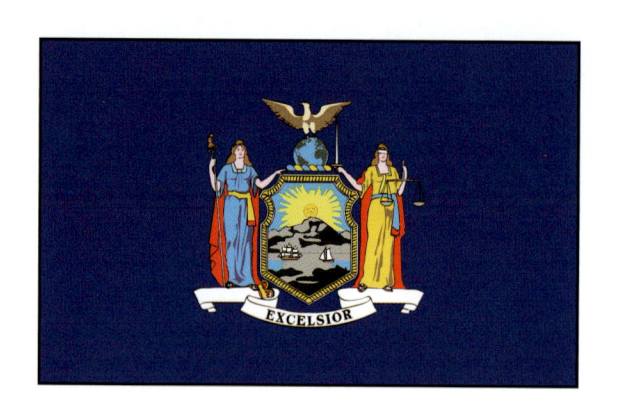

Pennsylvania

Motto: Virtue, Liberty, and Independence.
Nickname: Keystone State
Capital: Harrisburg
Known for: Forests, Valley Forge, Gettysburg, Liberty Bell, Independence Hall
Fun Fact: Thomas Edison's first successful experiment with electric lighting was conducted in Sunbury.

Ohio

Motto: With God, All Things are Possible.
Nickname: Buckeye State
Capital: Columbus
Known for: Rich Soil, Factories, and Birthplace of 8 U.S. Presidents
Fun Fact: Native Americans left over 6,000 burial mounds in the state.

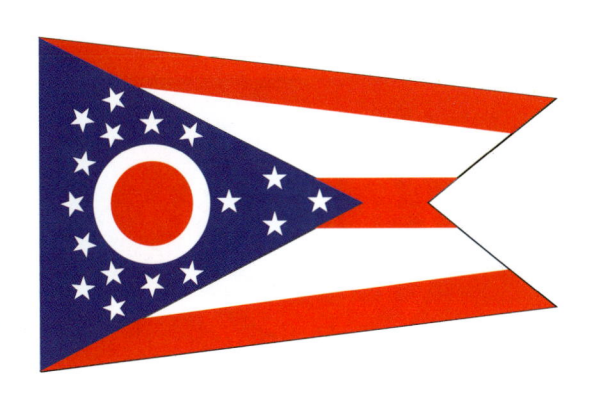

West Virginia

Motto: Montani Semper Liberi (which means "Mountaineers Are Always Free.")
Nickname: Mountain State
Capital: Charleston
Known for: Mountains, Wildlife, Coal, Harpers Ferry, Cass Scenic Railroad
Fun Fact: West Virginia is the only state to be designated by Presidential Proclamation.

Alabama

Motto: We Dare Maintain our Rights.
Nickname: The Heart of Dixie
Capital: Montgomery
Known for: Beaches, Cotton
Fun Fact: For a short time, Montgomery was the capital of the Confederate States of America.

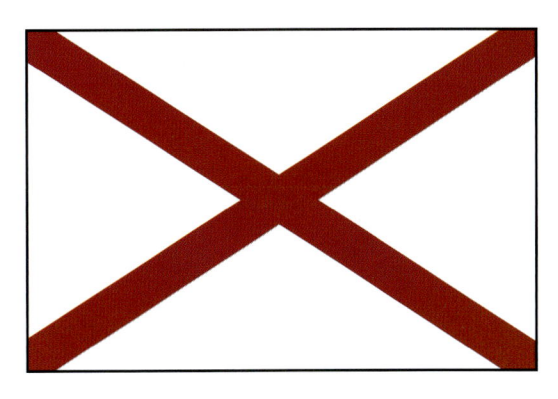

Virginia
Motto: Thus Always to Tyrants.
Nickname: The Old Dominion
Capital: Richmond
Known for: Tobacco, Jamestown Colony, Mountains, Coal
Fun Fact: The first peanuts grown in the U.S. were grown in Virginia.

Kentucky
Motto: United We Stand, Divided We Fall.
Nickname: The Bluegrass State
Capital: Frankfort
Known for: Kentucky Derby, Mammoth Caves
Fun Fact: Kentucky Bluegrass is not really blue, it's green. But its buds are a bluish-purple in the spring.

Tennessee
Motto: Agriculture and Commerce.
Nickname: The Volunteer State
Capital: Nashville
Known for: Great Smoky Mountains, Grand Ole Opry, Graceland
Fun Fact: A replica of Davy Crockett's log cabin stands on the banks of Limestone Creek.

North Carolina

Motto: While I Breathe, I Hope Ready in Soul and Resource.
Nickname: Tar Heel State
Capital: Raleigh
Known for: Beaches, Wright Brothers
Fun Fact: The first English child born in America was Virginia Dare in Roanoke.

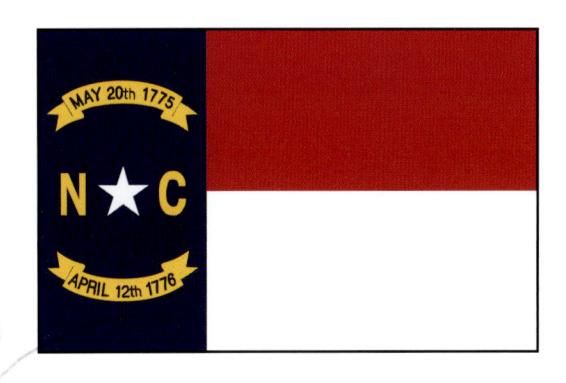

South Carolina

Motto: To Be, Rather Than to Seem.
Nickname: Palmetto State
Capital: Columbia
Known for: Myrtle Beach, Sea Turtles, Tobacco
Fun Fact: The first battle of the Civil War took place at Fort Sumter.

Georgia

Motto: Wisdom, Justice, and Moderation.
Nickname: The Peach State
Capital: Atlanta
Known for: Centennial Olympic Park, Peaches
Fun Fact: Georgia is the official state of the largemouth bass.

Glossary

cash crops (kash krahps): crops, such as tobacco or cotton, that are grown to be sold rather than for use by the farmer

coal (kohl): a hard, black substance used as a fuel

culture (KUHL-chur): the beliefs, customs, and arts of a particular group

dulcimer (DUHL-suh-mer): a stringed American folk instrument

forests (FOR-ists): a large, thick growth of trees and bushes

frontier (fruhn-TEER): a region on the margin of settled territory; a distant area where few people live

lumber (LUHM-ber): wooden boards or logs that have been cut for use

mining (mine-ing): taking minerals from a pit or hole in the earth

pioneers (pye-uh-NEERS) the first to settle in a territory

reclamation (rek-luh-MAY-shuhn): getting back something that was lost or taken away

rural (ROOR-uhl): relating to the country, country people or life, or agriculture

subsistence farmers (SUHB-sis-tens fahrm-urz): farmers who provide their families with the goods they require

tourism (TOOR-ism): the business of providing hotels, restaurants, and entertainment for people who are traveling

Index

Allegheny Mountains 6
Blue Ridge Mountains 6, 23
Cherokee 7, 8, 11, 12, 13, 14
coal 18, 19, 20
crafts 14
Cumberland Mountains 6
farmers 11, 16, 18
forests 6
Great Smoky Mountains 6
immigrants 10, 18
lumber 17, 20
mining 18, 19, 22
music 14, 24
poverty 20
storytelling 14, 15, 24
tourism 22

Show What You Know

1. What Native American tribe originally lived in the Appalachian region?
2. What were the main forms of entertainment among the European settlers in the Appalachian region?
3. What major industries were introduced to the region with the arrival of the railroad in the late 1800s?
4. How has the lumbering industry affected the present-day land in Appalachia?
5. How many people hike the Appalachian Scenic Trail each year?

Websites to Visit

www.arc.gov/index.asp
theallianceforappalachia.org
www.education.com/magazine/article/7_Sites_See_Appalachia

Author

Ellen Kavanagh Mitten has been teaching four and five year olds since 1995. She loves traveling and wouldn't mind visiting the beautiful Great Smoky Mountains. She and her family enjoy reading all sorts of books!

Meet The Author!
www.meetREMauthors.com

© 2015 Rourke Educational Media

All rights reserved. No part of this book may be reproduced or utilized in any form or by any means, electronic or mechanical including photocopying, recording, or by any information storage and retrieval system without permission in writing from the publisher.

www.rourkeeducationalmedia.com

PHOTO CREDITS: Title Page © Maridav; page 3 © Dean Fikar; page 4 © Vojkan Dimitrijievic; page 5 © mountainberryphoto; page 6, 25 © David Allen Photography; page 7 © Scott Prokop; page 8, 13, 16, 18 © Library of Congress; page 9 © Cookephotos, yuris, smereka; page 10 © Kenneth Keifer; page 11 © somchai rakin; page 12 © public domain; page 14 © tsmorton, rosta; page 15 © robert_s, Chursina Viktorila; page 17 © Chris Pecorano; page 19 © tinabelle; page 20 © Blue_Cutler; page 21 © Allalachin Regional Commission; page 22 © apelletr, Maridav; page 25 © Jason Patrick Ross; page 24 © gorillaimages, DinoZ

Edited by: Jill Sherman

Cover design by: Jen Thomas
Interior design by: Rhea Magaro

Library of Congress PCN Data

Appalachian Region / Ellen Mitten
(United States Regions)
ISBN 978-1-62717-674-3 (hard cover)
ISBN 978-1-62717-796-2 (soft cover)
ISBN 978-1-62717-913-3 (e-Book)
Library of Congress Control Number: 2014934382

Also Available as:
ROURKE'S e-Books

Printed in the United States of America, North Mankato, Minnesota